THE
MAGIC KALEIDOSCOPE

Sheila Black

ILLUSTRATED BY PAUL SELWYN

Ariel Books ◦ Andrews and McMeel ◦ Kansas City

ISBN: 0-8362-4227-0

Design: Diane Stevenson / Snap Haus Graphics

THE MAGIC KALEIDOSCOPE

Joey peered into the open window. Mr. Nostromo, the magician, was standing inside, holding a funny blue tube covered with silver stars, moons, and planets.

Joey caught his breath. He knew that it was wrong to spy. Yet ever since his mysterious neighbor had moved in, Joey had wanted a good look at him. Mr. Nostromo lifted the blue tube to his eye. The tube looked like a kaleidoscope. In fact, it was a kaleidoscope, for as Joey watched, Mr. Nostromo chanted:

Whirl down from afar
Kaleidoscope bright
Cast diamonds and stars
For my delight
Colors change, magic reveal
Make the real magical
And the magical real.

The magician turned the kaleidoscope tube clockwise three times. What happened next surprised Joey so much he almost fell over backwards. Mr. Nostromo's ordinary living room was transformed into the most amazing, fabulous room Joey had ever seen.

Mr. Nostromo's brown couch and beige armchairs shimmered with ever-changing colors and patterns. Diamonds and starbursts danced across the walls and the floors. The couch and the armchairs went from rainbow-colored stripes to plaid to polka dots in the twinkling of an eye. And the painting of flowers on the wall changed from orange to pink to purple to blue and back again.

Mr. Nostromo turned the tube of the kaleidoscope three more times. Now even more unbelievable things started to happen. The couch sprang to life and yodeled a cowboy song. The armchairs tap-danced around the room. The flowers in the painting leaped out of their frame, and performed a ballet on the coffee table, which giggled, "Stop! Stop! You're tickling!" Joey's eyes almost popped out of his head.

Mr. Nostromo put the kaleidoscope to his eye once more. Twisting the tube in the opposite direction from before, the magician chanted:

Whirl back to the stars
Kaleidoscope bright
Hide away and afar
Your spell of delight
Colors change back, magic conceal
Take away what is magical
And leave only what is real.

Instantly, everything went back to normal again. Joey ducked out of sight. Mr. Nostromo set the magic kaleidoscope down on the windowsill. Then the magician pulled on his raincoat, and went out—looking almost, but not quite, like an ordinary person.

As soon as Mr. Nostromo was gone, Joey stood up again. He couldn't resist picking up the magic kaleidoscope. He held it to his eye, and twisted the tube three times.

Whirl down from afar
Kaleidoscope bright
Cast diamonds and stars
For my delight

Joey stopped chanting, for that was all he could remember of Mr. Nostromo's spell. No sooner were the words out of Joey's mouth than his ordinary street of ordinary houses became the most amazing, incredible street imaginable. All the houses shimmered with color—blue, green, red, orange, purple, and bright yellow. So did the trees, and the lawns in front of the houses were no longer green, but checked and speckled and striped and polka-dotted. Even the sidewalk was streaked with rainbow colors.

Joey clapped his hands and laughed out loud. And he turned the tube of the magic kaleidoscope again.

The whole street sprang to life just as Mr. Nostromo's living room had. The flowers in the gardens bowed to one another, and began to talk in high, wispy voices. The trees spread out their branches and started to tango up and down the block. Even the houses swayed from side to side, and their windows and doors popped wide open.

"This is better than a Saturday morning cartoon!" Joey cried. But then the neighbors came running out. They weren't nearly as happy as Joey was with the spell the magic kaleidoscope had cast on their street.

"The world's gone crazy!" shouted Mr. Miller next door. "We better call the police!"

"We better call the firemen!" yelled Mrs. Popper.

"We better call the mayor!" shrieked Joey's mother.

"Oh, no!" Joey thought. He tried to turn the magic kaleidoscope backward. But he couldn't remember which way backward was. He couldn't remember the rest of Mr. Nostromo's spell either.

Now go away, go away,
Kaleidoscope of delight
Come back another day
With your colors so bright

He chanted. No, that wasn't the right spell. It only made matters worse. Now the neighbors all changed colors, too. Mr. Miller next door turned bright red, with green and yellow stripes. Mrs. Popper turned as purple as a grape. Even Joey's mother changed color. She became sky blue, with little silver stars all over. Then even gravity lost its pull, for people and animals started to float into the air like helium balloons.

"Oh, no!" wailed Joey. "What do I do now?" Luckily, just then he spotted Mr. Nostromo walking down the street. "Help! Help!" Joey cried. "Make the magic STOP!"

Mr. Nostromo stretched his arm up for the kaleidoscope. He quickly chanted the proper spell. The kaleidoscope colors began to fade. Little by little, everything settled back to its proper place.

"Hello," Mr. Miller said to Mrs. Popper. "Nice weather we're having." "Sure is," said Joey's mother. "Not too hot for July." Joey breathed a sigh of relief. Clearly, none of the grown-ups could even remember what had happened. Then he saw Mr. Nostromo looking at him very, very sternly.

"Where did you get MY kaleidoscope?" the magician said.

"I took it from your windowsill, sir."

"I thought so." Mr. Nostromo's eyes flashed. "I ought to turn you into a horned toad or a spotted newt or a —"

"Please don't!" Joey pleaded. "My mother would never get over it."

"No," Mr. Nostromo said. "I daresay she wouldn't. But what you did was wrong."

"I know," said Joey. "I'm sorry."

Mr. Nostromo ignored his apology. "Report to my house at ten o'clock sharp tomorrow morning."

Joey gulped. "Yes, sir."

At ten o'clock the next morning, Joey stood at Mr. Nostromo's front door. He knew he should knock, but he was scared. What would Mr. Nostromo do? Then Joey saw the sign on the door. "Help wanted," it said. "One magician's assistant needed. Must be curious, quick-witted, and adventurous. Must also be OBEDIENT. Apply in person only."

Joey knocked on the door. It swung softly open, and there stood Mr. Nostromo. "Joey!" he said. "Come in. I've been expecting you."